HUMPTY DUMPTY JR.
HARDBOILED DETECTIVE

in

THE MYSTERY OF MERLIN AND THE GRUESOME GHOST

by: Nate Evans and Paul Hindman
Illustrated by: Vince Evans and Nate Evans

SOURCEBOOKS
Jabberwocky
AN IMPRINT OF SOURCEBOOKS

Published by Sourcebooks Jabberwocky, an imprint of Sourcebooks, Inc.
P.O. Box 4410, Naperville, Illinois 60567-4410
(630) 961-3900
Fax: (630) 961-2168
www.sourcebooks.com

Cataloging-in-Publication data is on file with the publisher.

Printed and bound in the United States of America.
VP 10 9 8 7 6 5 4 3 2 1

For my daughter
Dakota Rachel
—New York Fashion Kitten
—Paul

For my mom, Rusty,
Thank you for a lifetime of encouragement,
wisdom, and wonderful conversations.
With love,
Nate

For Laurie,
Who makes me laugh and brightens my day.
You are my eternal source of inspiration.
Love,
Vince

TABLE OF CONTENTS

Chapter 1
Gloom and Doom

Once Upon a Crime:
  There was a detective.
  Me.
  Humpty Dumpty Jr., Hardboiled Detective.
  I'm a good egg who always cracks the case.
  I live and work in the city.

My city.
New Yolk, New Yolk.
A crazy, dangerous, beautiful town.

We were standing at my office window, watching the raindrops splat like water balloons.

Me and my sidekick, Rat.

And, man, is he ever a sidekicker.

We were having the argument. *Again.*

"No way!" Rat shouted. "No way I'm going to school!"

His angry voice was as loud as the thunder shaking the building.

"Listen, kiddo," I patiently stated, *again,* "that's our deal. You only get to be my partner if you live with Patty Cake and go to school."

This kid, Rat, had recently been living on the streets.

I met him on a case: The Fiendish Flapjack Flop.

"You know Patty makes me take baths," Rat said. "Baths are for wimps!

"Have you ever sat in boiling bathwater for so long that you wound up wrinkleder than Patty Cake's knees?"

I replied, "I've been boiled once, thank you; that's enough for me. And just for the record, that's not exactly the story I hear from Patty."

At bath time, Rat actually whimpers and whines, then jumps out the window in his underwear and climbs onto the roof.

Poor Patty has to coax the kid in with a plate of donuts. He barely sticks his foot in the tub before announcing his bath is done.

"Okay, wise guy," Rat snapped. "Totally ignore my pain."

Rat looked completely different than the day I met him: back then he was a scrawny, filthy runt.

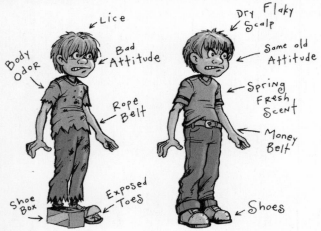

Now, he's scrubbed clean, with a slick haircut (except he messes it up as soon as he steps out of Patty's bakery).

And spanking new clothes (complete with pockets, buttons, and working zippers).

Rat hollered, "I just want to be your partner and solve mysteries."

It was gloomy and dark that morning.

The noises of the street (usually shriller than a parade of anteaters playing saxophones) were muffled and dull.

It was the kind of weather that seeps into your guts and makes your spirits all damp and soggy.

Listening to Rat harp on the same old tune wasn't helping.

But, life goes on. I picked up today's paper:

MAYOR FLUTTERBUTT BUSTED!
Crime Boss "Royal" Flush At Large

NYPD Lieutenant Rhino Rosebriar of the 54th Precinct arrested NYC Mayor Flutterbutt in a dawn raid!

As most of the city officials arrived at City Hall this morning, they were met by Lt. Rosebriar and a paddy wagon. The officials were nabbed for bribery, theft, and mob connections.

Lt. Rosebriar commented at the arrest: "These guys are all connected to the Potty Mouth Gang. We suspect Boss 'Royal' Flush is behind this whole Organization. But no one knows who Flush is! He's the baddest baddie of 'em all, and he's just a shadow within a shadow. But don't worry. We'll get 'im."

I've had plenty of run-ins with the Potty Mouth Gang. Knock-Out Louie, Toothless Moe, and the rest. Dumb as ogres (which is an insult to ogres). But their Boss is a brilliant, mysterious figure, the looming phantom behind some of the biggest heists in the city.

If only we knew who the rat was!

I jumped as something pounded our office door like a jackhammer.

Rat shouted, excited, "My first customer! I'll handle it!"

He ran to the door and threw it open.

From the shell-shocking clamor of our visitor's knock, I was expecting at least a rock-troll, possibly a giant. But standing at the open door was a frail, pale girl.

She was shivering, soaked, her hair dripping rivers. She leaned weakly against the doorframe.

Then she collapsed into Rat's arms, moaning, "Help!"

Rat turned to me, with a 'yuck-it's-a-girl' expression.

"It's for you," he said.

Chapter 2
The Frozen Lily

We moved the shivering girl to my comfy desk chair.

I wrapped her in a big blanket.

Rat crouched in the farthest corner, glaring at her like she was some kind of dripping alien fungus.

"Whatsa matter?" I asked her. "You look like you've seen a ghost!"

"The ghost!" she screamed, clutching my arm tightly.

"Really?" I asked. "A real ghost?"

She wiped her nose on my tie, took a breath and said, "A ghost...in glowing armor...wandering the halls, and classrooms..."

I said, "Where—?"

"...the magic workshops, the courtyard..."

"Yeah, but—"

"...the bat cages, the bathrooms...clanking and rattling and freaking everybody out!"

"Yeah, kid. But where?"

"My school."

"Gimme a name."

"Merlin's Institute for the Knowledge of Everything!"

I asked, "And whadda we call you?"

"Lily," the girl said, shivering a bit less. "Princess Lily."

I'd already noticed the small tiara in her sopping hair. It looked like a dime-store crown.

Rat sneered from his corner, "Princess! Of what?"

"My father's Prince Balto. That makes me Princess Lily," the girl stated.

Except for her cheap tiara, Princess Lily was dressed like any average girl: A navy blue skirt with silver stars, white blouse and stockings, a blazer too big. Old, worn-out penny loafers.

She looked to be about Rat's age.

I handed Lily cookies and a mug of hot chocolate, and said, "So there's a ghost at Merlin's Institute?"

Lily nodded. She nibbled her cookie. "Poppa's really sick," she finally whispered. "From…the ghost. Last night he went to fight it, 'cause Merlin wasn't doing anything. I found Poppa this morning…in a hallway. He won't wake up!"

Hands shaking, she sipped her cocoa, then pointed at Rat. "Why's *he* here?"

Rat blurted, "I *work* with him. *We're* trying to find out why *you're* here!"

The princess nodded. "I want to hire you."

She glanced down sadly. "I was so excited to get into Merlin's Institute," she said. "To study with Merlin the Magician himself!"

Rat inched closer to the desk, his expression a mixture of disgust and curiosity.

Lily went on, "But everything's gone wrong… poor Poppa…"

I asked, "Any more clues about the ghost?"

"It walks through walls," said the princess. "And it moans."

"Does it say anything?" I asked.

Lily sniffled and said, "Sometimes…Mostly it moans…But…some-times it says…"

"Go on."

"'GIVE ME MY MAGIC!'" Lily shrieked.

Chapter 3
Journey Underground

Rat said, "Okay, so about our fee…"

"I've only got—" Lily began.

"Zip it," I said, glaring at Rat.

I grabbed my wand. I also swooped my parachute-sized green umbrella from its ogre-foot stand.

It wasn't very far to the subway station. We'd get there through this storm even if we'd have to sail there!

We made it to the subway and started down the stairs. As I lowered the umbrella, I noticed Rat standing a few steps above me. He was, for the record, very wet.

Startled, I said, "Why didn't you get under the umbrella?"

Rat, shaking himself off, said, "This counts as bath time. I'm clean!"

I knew the real reason. "Look, she's just a girl," I said. "Well, she's actually a princess, but royalty are just people. No big deal, okay? And she's our client."

Rat caught up with me, and we both caught up with Lily.

Our subway train was waiting, the steamy, wet passengers and their steamy, wet clothing fogging up the windows.

"Let's jump on," I said.

After squeezing, poking, plowing, and punching, I got the kids and myself (and my enormous umbrella) onto the smelly "D" train to 5th Ave.

"So, how long have you been at Merlin's school?" I asked Lily as we seated ourselves.

"Just a few days. At first Merlin wouldn't let me in. But Poppa talked him into it. We sold our castle to get the tuition. Plus, he took a job at the school, for no money. Poppa…" She sniffled again.

"It's just me and Poppa. Momma died when I was born. Poppa tries so hard…"

Rat asked, "Who is this Merlin dude anyway?"

"He's the greatest wizard ever!" Lily said. "He was asleep for a thousand years and then came here to start his school. He's totally amazing!"

Irritated, Rat looked at me for the real story.

"She's right," I said. "About ten years ago, this big sword (stuck in a stone and anvil) miraculously appeared in New Yolk. Next thing, Merlin blew into town. He announced that he was looking for a king. Whoever could pull the sword from the stone was supposed to be the Big Cheese."

Lily chimed in, "But nobody could do it. Merlin's still waiting."

I continued, "So Merlin started his school, and it was a hit. Princes from all over the world showed up, to try the sword, and to study with Merlin."

The loudspeaker in the car squawked: "Broad…smsh…smhr krrrkkkk, transfers to Bonx, Burplyn, schmmch shchmknm, kk…5th Avenue."

"That's us," I said.

We got off the train and climbed to 5th Ave.

Fat drops of rain plunked into puddles, splashing mud fountains everywhere.

"The school is Merlin's actual castle from England," I continued as we walked. This time Rat joined us under the umbrella.

I said, "Merlin brought it to New Yolk City by magic. It just plopped out of nowhere, right between the Giggleheim Art Museum and the Swine Gas Works."

Speaking of which, as we approached the school, the stench of the Gas Works made me wanna trade in my fedora hat for a gas mask.

We crossed the Institute's drawbridge over the moat.

Two enormous suits of armor blocked the front door with bronze battle-axes bigger than Liberty's torch.

I stepped forward. "What's this?"

A mechanical voice boomed from behind one of the guard's slatted visors, "Dis is 'no dice.'"

Lily said, "I'm a student here."

The other guard growled in a tinny falsetto at Lily, "Youse can go in, but ix-nay on the egg-yay."

What was it with these guys' voices? One sounded like a robot, the other like Mickey Mouse.

I retorted, "But we're here to see Merlin! The Headmaster. About the ghost!"

The first tough guy stepped forward, brandishing his axe. "Nuts to you. And da squirt."

Both guards bellowed with laughter.

I persisted, "This 'squirt' is actually rich and famous, royalty!"

The guard on the left looked at Rat. "Yeah, so why do ya look so broke?"

I said, "He's in disguise! He likes to keep a low profile."

One guard squeaked to the other, "Da boss said let rich kids in."

The other guard said, "He got magic? Da boss said let in rich kids wid magic."

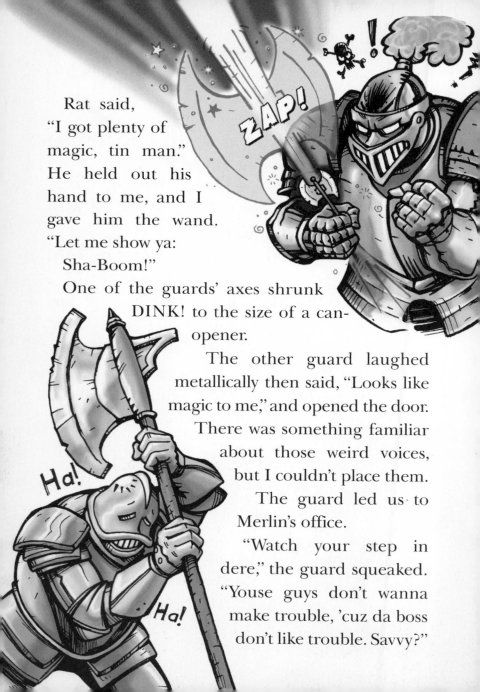

Rat said, "I got plenty of magic, tin man." He held out his hand to me, and I gave him the wand. "Let me show ya: Sha-Boom!"

One of the guards' axes shrunk DINK! to the size of a can-opener.

The other guard laughed metallically then said, "Looks like magic to me," and opened the door. There was something familiar about those weird voices, but I couldn't place them.

The guard led us to Merlin's office.

"Watch your step in dere," the guard squeaked. "Youse guys don't wanna make trouble, 'cuz da boss don't like trouble. Savvy?"

Chapter 4
The Musty Magician

Two more lunkheads in lead suits guarded Merlin's office. We breezed by and barged in.

The Old Geezer jumped at our rude entrance.

Merlin's face was pale and wrinkled, his skin leathery.

His white hair and beard were yellowed with age like old books. Tangled and ragged.

He smelled funky, like dirty wet socks.

He looked like a laundry bag with feet.

I tipped my hat and said, "Name's Dumpty. Private Eye."

I flashed my PI badge at him as I gave his office the once-over.

The joint was chock-full of claustrophobic clutter—a catastrophic collection of all things crazy and creepy.

Blood-stained suits of armor. Scraggly stuffed creatures from alligators to unicorns. Lab tables with beakers and fuming vials stinking like green puke.

I pricked the end of the unicorn's horn with my pinky.

"Don't touch that!" Merlin commanded, slapping my hand away. "What are you doing here?"

I said, "We're here to look into your little mystery."

Rat snapped back, "We're here to smash your ghost, is all! Get a clue."

"But there is no ghost!" Merlin stated.

Lily meekly piped up, "If there's no ghost, why is my father sick?"

Rat added, "Yeah. He musta got a big bad 'boo-boo' from your ghost!"

Merlin huffed impatiently. "Spoiled cafeteria food, alas, put him in the infirmary. There was no ghost going 'boo'!"

The magician stood to his full height and glared with sudden electric eyes at Rat. "And who are you?"

The wrinkled old toad was crowding me. I'm the detective here. I ask the questions. But I'd run out. Once Merlin denied there even was a ghost, I had nowhere to go.

I said, "Er, we came to enroll Rat here."

Rat sputtered, "Egg-roll me? What??"

Merlin snorted. "The Institute is for special students. This boy is obviously not royalty, has no money, no manners—and no place in this school!"

"As for the so-called ghost," Merlin said. "I do not want any help."

"So, where's the sword?" I said. "Did you ever find your king?"

Merlin stood tall, all dramatic and posing, his stance wide like he was straddling the chasms of history.

"I am the keeper of the Sword Excalibur!" Merlin said. "I am the guardian of the king, who will return."

I'm tellin' ya, all I needed was some popcorn.

Merlin stood before the thick velvet curtain behind the desk.

With a flourish, he swept the curtain away, revealing a magnificent sword. In a stone. And anvil.

Excalibur glowed. Shining a clean, clear gold.

I heard Lily gasp. "*Amazing!*"

Merlin exclaimed, "Gadzooks! The Sword awakens." The Sword brightened, sparkled.

"It's the *king*," Merlin continued. "Here in this room! The Sword is shining to welcome the Once and Future King."

Merlin's gaze shifted from the Sword to Rat.

"It's you."

Merlin grabbed Rat's collar.

"Try it, boy. Try to draw the Sword."

Merlin pushed Rat forward.

Rat struggled. "What the—?"

Lily said excitedly, "Oh Rat, you might be the new King Arthur!"

"What are you talking about?"

Merlin shrieked, "One thousand years ago, a young boy drew this same Sword from the stone. He was the rightful king! Arthur. It is foretold! He shall return!"

Owl-eyed, Merlin inspected Rat. "Tell me, boy. Just who are you?"

"I'm Rat!"

I stepped in. "We don't really know who he is."

The lights in Merlin's eyes jumped 2000 Volts.

Merlin barked: "How old are you, lad?"

Rat said, "Go figure."

I volunteered, "We guess he's around ten."

Merlin crowed, "Of course! Right when the Sword appeared! The Sword announced your birth!"

Merlin waved his hand dramatically toward Excalibur. "Draw the Sword, lad. It calls you."

Merlin loomed over Rat, a madman's glimmer lighting his face.

Rat tentatively touched the Sword.

Nothing happened.

He pulled on the hilt.

Nothing happened.

"But…" Merlin stuttered, "…try harder, boy!"

Rat tried again.

No deal.

"I knew I wasn't some old king," Rat muttered.

Merlin, frustrated, fluttered the tail of his ragged beard. His face lit up again.

"Of course!" he exclaimed, rubbing his hands. "The lad is nowhere near ready!

"Certainly, the boy will be enrolled!" Merlin announced. "He shall be tutored here, by me! In days of yore, it was only after my training that Arthur pulled Excalibur free!"

Rat said, "So, what am I king of?"

"Possibly the world," said Merlin. "The power of the Sword is unfathomable—there's never been a weapon like it."

My shell sorta tingled at the way Merlin purred 'weapon.'

Princess Lily meekly asked, "Sir, may I try the Sword?"

Merlin looked impatiently at the girl. He scolded, "Certainly NOT! You're the janitor's daughter!"

He closed the curtains, hiding the Sword.

Merlin turned to Rat again, saying, "We shall discover without question just who you are."

I said, "So, Merlin, about your ghost? Do yourself a favor. Lemme look into it."

"No, no, no. There is no ghost," he sputtered. "I regret to insist…though you are somehow attached to this important person…"

Merlin glared, "…If you are not out of here, very shortly…I shall have you dragged out."

"Okay, okay," I said. "I'm rolling."

The old wizard kindly patted Rat and said, "You shall begin classes immediately. You'll move into the dormitory today."

"Well, kid," I said to Rat as we left Merlin's office, "if the cards you're holding win you a spiky hat and a ritzy kingdom, then I'm happy for ya."

I said, "But no way am I gonna let that dust-bag Merlin keep me outta here. Lily's our client, not him."

I looked around for the princess, and found her standing, trancelike, before Merlin's closed door.

I heard her mutter dreamily, "Excalibur…"

She turned to Rat. "You're so lucky, Rat."

"Hey," he said. "Call me 'King Rat.'"

Chapter 5
Nurse Punnymany

We went to the infirmary to see if Lily's dad was feeling better.

"A janitor, huh?" Rat said. "So, you must be 'Princess Plunger.'"

Lily blushed.

I said, "Nothin' wrong being a janitor. And, you're forgetting—this janitor had the guts to stand alone against a gruesome ghost!"

Lily led us up more stone steps, worn and smooth like dark slabs of polished butter.

We passed through more rooms and hallways, ancient, musty, and damp.

She parted a heavy curtain, and we entered a large area, lined with cots.

Lily whispered, "Here's Poppa."

We followed her over to the nearest bed.

The man lying there would have been handsome, had his face not been as pale and wooden as white oak.

Prince Balto had fine cheekbones and a sharp jawline; but, overall, his face was gentle.

A sharp whisper broke the silence, and the three of us jumped. "Lily, child, 'oo is this crowd?"

I wouldn't call just Rat and me a *crowd*.

We turned and stood face-to-face with a tall, furry rabbit in a nurse's outfit.

"Nurse Punnymany," Lily said, "we came to visit my poppa."

"Well," Nurse Punnymany whispered, "won't 'arm your father none, Ducky."

I offered my hand to the rabbit nurse. She shook it with gusto and said, "Why would you want to come to this place, what's 'aunted and all?"

"Tell me what haunts it," I said.

"Well," the rabbit said, "I'm certain I dunno. And cursed if Old Windbag 'as nary a peck of a pickled notion."

"You mean Merlin?" I asked.

"'Oo else? All of them what was attacked say Merlin was nowhere to be seen, nor come to help, scream as they might. And then 'e told 'em it must'a been sump'n they ate what made 'em ill and seein' things.

"This one 'ere is the first victim," Nurse Punnymany stated, placing her paw at the foot of a cot next to Balto's.

"'E come in, just as you see 'im. Still an' cold as Death. Dugal Farthing. Fine boy. Royalty, 'e is."

I asked, "Where are his parents?"

"Ah," the nurse sighed, "'alf a world away, at 'ome in Ireland. And, don'tcher know, his magical Nibs 'imself, Merlin, just wrote 'em a simple faerie-gram wot sez, 'Yer poor lad fell ill with the stomach flu, not to worry.'"

Nurse Punnymany patted Dugal's foot. "Poor lad. Don'tcher know 'e's mightily strong with the magic, 'e is. It don't surprise me if 'e didn't put up a mighty fight when 'e saw that ghosty."

"How do you know there's a ghost?"

"Cor," Punnymany exclaimed, "don'tcher know all o' the poor childings 'oo come in 'ere, all wobbled and shooken, each one moaning about the ghosty?

None of 'em was as sick as these two, and were fit the follerin' day. But, sure, nothing but a real ghosty coulda put them each in such a fright."

Suddenly, Dugal's body bolted upright. His eyes were closed. He screamed, "No!"

Then Dugal roared, "Leave my magic alone!" and fell PLOP on his back, still as rock.

Nurse Punnymany rushed to Dugal's side.

I asked Lily, "He was talking to the ghost, wasn't he?"

The princess nodded. "That's what they say the ghost moans—'Where's My Magic?'" Lily laid her face against her father's chest and sobbed, "Oh, Poppa."

I was mad. 'No ghost', my butt! Oh, we're coming in, and we're grabbing this ghost!

A thousand Merlins couldn't keep me away.

Chapter 6
Morphing Madness

I told Lily we'd be back soon. We left her sitting miserably, holding her dad's limp hand.

Rat and I headed back to my office.

"I've got to figure a way to case that joint," I said.

Rat said, "So, go in disguise!"

"Great eggheads think alike."

Rat asked, "Why don't you go as a new student? Then I won't have to. I can't even read, and I'm supposed to study with that cruddy smelly cheese, Merlin?"

"Don't worry, kid," I said. "You'll do fine. We both gotta be there to find clues. Partners, remember?

"Besides, Merlin may be cheesy, but he's also a great wizard. If he thinks you're the king, then you might be. You better just play along."

I wasn't looking forward to telling Patty Cake that Rat couldn't live with her anymore (because he might just be some long lost King of the World).

I said, "We'll swing by Patty's and pack up your gear to move into the dorm."

At the office, I went to my Cupboard of Disguises and rummaged. "Hmmm...you know what the Merlin Institute needs?" I said. "A new janitor."

"Yeah!" Rat said.

"Not sure I have a Janitor costume...I wonder if I can fake it?"

"Let me do it."

"Choose my disguise?"

"Change you, with magic. If you're gonna fool Merlin, you need a great disguise!"

"Well, you got me there, kid. And when an egg's beaten, it stays beaten."

"Cool," Rat said. "So, cough it up."

"Nothing fancy," I said, handing him the wand. "Just standard janitor."

"And a mustache," Rat said.

"A mustache?"

"Yeah, a big, floppy mustache."

I stood still, waiting for disaster to strike.

It did.

"Sha-Boom!"

POOF!

I was a toilet!

With a mustache!

"Oops. Heh heh," Rat snickered. "Sorry!"

"Sha-Boom!"

POOF!

Then I was myself again…except my eyes (and my mustache) were on the back of my head!

"Oops," Rat said. "Oops."

"Sha-Boom!"

POOF!

I was the Statue of Liberty! With a mustache!

I muttered, "You keep getting the mustache right, kid."

"I can do this," Rat growled.

POOF!

I was myself again.

With a big, bushy mustache.

"That's enough!" I grabbed the wand. I went back to my Cupboard of Disguises. "See, maybe studying with Merlin won't be so bad. You're a natural with the wand, kid, but you got plenty to learn."

I pulled out some old overalls I'd worn working undercover at Old MacDonald's Fairy Dairy.

They'd have to do.

Rat giggled, trying to muffle the sound.

"How do I look?" I asked, turning to Rat.

"You look good in a mustache."

Chapter 7
Of Swords and Snotswarths

Rat and I entered the school with no guff from the guards this time.

Merlin appeared before us, and placed his arm around Rat. "I have just the class for you."

Then Merlin saw me.

"Who are you? Haven't we met?" he asked suspiciously.

I ducked my head, mumbled some double-talk, "substitute janitor," "last minute."

Merlin grabbed my mustache and yanked it. "YOW!"

"Hmmm," Merlin hummed, then curtly commanded, "Get to work!"

Merlin strode off, Rat in tow, saying, "Lad, are you prepared to claim your Destiny?"

Rat mumbled, "Whatever."

I quickly slipped up the stairs to the infirmary to check on Lily.

Nurse Punnymany gently told the princess, "Don't fret, chicky. I'll tend yer poor Da. Go on about yer day. It's what yer Da would want, don'tcher know."

We left, and I filled Lily in on the new plan.

As she led me down to the janitor's closet, I asked her how I looked.

She took my disguise in, head to toe, and said, sweetly, "Er, you look good in a mustache."

I grabbed a mop and bucket out of the closet, then escorted Lily to her next class: sword-fighting.

Lily said, "But I can't sword-fight!"

I said, "Well, that's why they have classes, to teach you."

"Yeah, but I don't like sword-fighting."

As we entered the classroom, we saw that Rat was there, too.

Merlin introduced him to the teacher just as we

arrived. The kids put on their dueling gear, swinging their practice swords wildly.

I sized up the sword-fight instructor.

He was one of Merlin's armored tanks.

The instructor barked, "Teams," in a metallic voice
like the other guards', but more like gargling un-
derwater.

Suddenly, a kid at the back of the class cried out:
"I think I'm gonna—"

He heaved all over the wall, spouting like a
whale. "Oooooh," he moaned, frowning at the mess.
"I don't remember eating that!"

The other princes exploded in laughter.

"Well?" Merlin's sharp voice snapped at my ear.
"Clean that up!"

Uh, right. I'm the janitor.

Merlin strode from the room.

Holding my breath as much as I could, I went to work cleaning up the kid's whale-spew.

Gross.

As I worked, I heard the instructor shouting, "Position One, youse brats. Points up, points up!"

He clanked around the room.

Something about that voice, echoing and booming as it was, also rang familiar.

A strong accent from the Bonx across the river.

I decided I'd have to try to decode these voices.

I sneaked my electronic notebook out of my pocket and set it to 'RECORD'.

"Dat's right!" he said. "De udder way," he instructed.

"You," he said, pointing at Lily, "and you," pointing at a snobby-looking prince.

The prince looked at least six years older than little Lily.

He also looked pretty handy with a sword.

Lily's opponent snapped his weapon up and announced: "Prince Cyril Snotswarth."

"Princess L-Lily," Lily said and saluted the same way.

"Mix it up," the instructor hollered.

The prince danced to and fro, back and forth and around Lily. He smacked her with his practice sword and laughed.

BONK!

Lily wildly swung her enormous blade; it swerved like a drunken flyswatter in a tornado. Prince Snotswarth taunted, "You shouldn't even be here." BONK! "You should be cleaning for a house of dwarfs." SMACK! "Or locked in a tower, helpless, waiting for someone to rescue you." SWAT!

I was getting steamed. I thought about dunking the prince's head in barf when Rat suddenly jumped into the fray.

"Hey, Snot-blower," Rat said.

The prince snarled and swung his sword.

Rat dodged the blow, threw his huge sword at Snotswarth's head, and tackled the Prince.

Rat grabbed Cyril's leg and chomped down!

Snotswarth, for the record, screeched like a bucket full of alley cats.

The sword instructor guffawed behind his armored helm.

Who were these tin-plated clowns? They were as fishy as canned tuna!

What was really going on here at Merlin's Institute?

I'm tellin' ya—Humpty the janitor was gonna clean up this entire mess. A sure bet.

Call your bookie.

Chapter 8
The Gruesome Ghost

Lily fell asleep in the infirmary during dinner.

It had been a long, grueling day for the poor kid.

I tucked her into a cot near her dad then turned to Rat. "You ready for our first ghost-watch?"

"Better give me the wand, Round Man," he suggested.

"Right." I handed the magic to the magic-user.

We searched hallways and stairwells and behind tapestries for hours.

Then, a CLUNK down a dorm hallway.

"Duck," I whispered.

Rounding the corner were an armored goon and Prince Snotswarth. I pulled out my notebook to record the guard if he spoke.

They stopped at Cyril's door, and I heard the guard grunt in a mechanical drone, "Dat's right, youse don't wanna go anywheres. Nobody leaves. Da boss says it's risky. And da boss knows trouble. Savvy?"

Cyril meekly closed his door, and the guard clanked off.

"Dude," Rat whispered.

"Right. Smells fishy."

I made a note of that.

We continued our ghost-watch.

Then, finally, checking out a classroom on the 5th floor, we heard it.

First, a faint moaning, echoing down the halls.

Then, louder. Closer. Closer.

We quietly moved to the classroom door.

Then, down the hall, we saw a steadily glowing green light. Brighter. Brighter.

I looked at Rat. "Ready?"

Rat nodded. We both leapt into the hall.

There, looming over us, his armor glowing brightly ghoulish, was The Ghost.

Demonic red eyes blazed from his visor.

His horned helmet was a huge skull surrounded by crackling flame.

The ghost waved a thrumming, sparking thing in his hand. Kinda like a large flashlight.

My shell tingled all over.

Rat yelled, "Sha-Boom!"

Rat's magic passed right through the ghost, crackling into a thousand fireworks against the far wall.

I groaned, "Magic's a no-go."

The ghost raised his arms and plodded closer on silent feet.

It roared, "Draw the Sword! The Sword!"

Then it turned and walked through the wall.

Chapter 9
Lord Feathergrimm

"There's got to be a way to get more info on this ghost," I said.

The next morning we stood in Lily and her father's basement apartment. I'd slept in Prince Balto's room, Rat in his dormitory.

Lily called from inside her bedroom, where she was dressing, "I think I know someone who can help."

We'd just finished breakfast, and Lily wanted a bath and a change of clothes.

I took in the tiny place, clean and tidy, but poorly furnished with unmatched wooden chairs and a mangy sofa.

Rat whispered, "What kind of a princess lives in a basement?"

"Easy, kid," I said softly. "Don't forget, it wasn't too long ago that you lived in a basement. And you might be a king."

On a rickety end table stood two framed snapshots, one of Prince Balto holding the baby Lily. The other one was of a gorgeous, regal woman in flowing robes.

She had a sparkle in her eyes to outshine starlight.

"That's my mom," Lily said behind us.

She took the frame and pointed to a ring on her mother's thumb. "See this?"

She replaced the pic on the table.

Reaching to her neck, she said, "This is the only thing I have of hers."

She pulled a silver chain from behind her shirt.

Dangling from the chain was a swanky gold ring.

The one worn by Lily's mom.

Even Rat came closer to see it.

"Whoa," he said.

The ring was golden. But, deep in the gold, encircling the ring, slithered a finely etched silver dragon.

The dragon's eyes sparkled brilliantly—two flawless diamonds.

"That's swell, all right," I said. "Fit for a princess."

Lily sighed and returned the ring inside her shirt, then said, "Let's go."

She led us down a maze of hallways into a huge library.

Inside, we found an old man in an old black robe, scribbling away with a quill ink pen.

He didn't seem much younger than 120 years old.

White hair spouted like foamy fountains out each side of his otherwise bald head.

On closer inspection, I noticed his white hair actually grew out his ears.

His face was lined all over, like fine print on newspaper.

Smack on this guy's cheek was a gigantic wart.

The old guy looked up from his work and smiled. "Lily!"

"Hi, Lord Feathergrimm," said Lily. She turned to Rat and me. "He's the head librarian. He knows everything."

Lord Feathergrimm put down his quill, slapping dandruff and dust off his wrinkled robes.

Lily introduced us.

"And how's your father?" the librarian asked.

Lily looked down and shook her head.

I patted her shoulder then said, "Well, Lord Feathergrimm, we're here to get the skinny on the ghost."

"The 'skinny'?" he asked.

"Sure," I said. "The scoop."

"He needs more facts," said Lily.

Lord Feathergrimm sat down, picked up his quill, and tapped his nose. "I'm quite unable to make sense of anything."

I said, "The ghost moans about magic. Who would haunt Merlin's Institute, looking for his magic?"

Rat said, "Don't forget, last night the ghost was yelling about 'the Sword', too."

"So the ghost wants Excalibur!" said Lily.

I asked, "Any chance King Arthur's the ghost?"

Feathergrimm, startled, knocked over his inkwell, spilling puddles of blue ink over everything.

"Never!" the librarian stated, dabbing at the ink puddles with a handkerchief. "Arthur was a good man. Even if his spirit were haunting the Institute, he wouldn't hurt anyone. His dream was to protect others. 'Might for right, instead of might makes right.'"

"Huh?" Rat asked.

Lily explained, "It means the strong have to help the weak."

Lord Feathergrimm dabbed his forehead with his ink-stained handkerchief. "Before Arthur pulled Excalibur from the stone and became king, it was a dark and terrible time in Britain. Brutal knights roamed the land, taking what they wanted, doing as they pleased.

"Arthur changed all that. He got the knights to behave themselves and help folk in trouble."

King Ar...

Lily added, dreamily, "And the greatest Knights of the Round Table became heroes: Sir Galahad, Sir Gawain, Sir Percival."

Feathergrimm again dabbed his face with his inky hanky, unaware of the mess he made.

He continued, "At its peak, Camelot was a glorious realm of peace and plenty."

I said, "But Arthur and Merlin had enemies, right?"

"Of course. There were terrible villains," the librarian stated. "The Queen of Air and Darkness, called Morgan Le Fay. And Mordred…"

"Arthur's only child," Lily said softly.

"The Black Prince," Feathergrimm said. "Mordred destroyed the Round Table. Then he and Arthur killed each other. The Final Battle. Camelot fell, and the Dark Age returned."

Rat exclaimed, "How come King Arthur didn't totally mow everybody down in one blow, if Excalibur is supposed to be this mega-super-powerful weapon?"

"I believe," Lord Feathergrimm stated softly, "the king hesitated to use the Sword in that way. Especially against his own son."

Feathergrimm sighed. He absentmindedly dabbed the spilled ink puddles on the desk, then dabbed his cheeks and neck.

"Dude," Rat whispered. "Shouldn't we tell him he looks like a blueberry with a wart?"

"Shh," I said, then to Feathergrimm, "Fill us in on Merlin coming to New Yolk, Excalibur, and all."

"Well," Lord Feathergrimm began, "you know that Merlin lived in the age of Arthur, over one thousand years ago. He was young Arthur's tutor and led him to the drawing of the Sword Excalibur."

Feathergrimm said, his blue face dripping, "Just before Camelot fell, Morgan Le Fay defeated Merlin in a wizard's duel, then trapped him in a crystal cave."

Lily slowly stated, "It's so sad. Merlin couldn't help King Arthur. Arthur was killed, and Excalibur disappeared."

Feathergrimm perked up. "Then, incredibly, the Sword Excalibur appeared on the shores of New Yolk, this little island (remember, Britain, too, is an island). Ten years ago.

"When the Sword appeared, Morgan's spell was miraculously broken, and Merlin was released from the crystal cave.

"Learning that the Sword Excalibur was in New Yolk, he jumped the first cosmic whirlwind and swirled across the Atlantic, his entire Celtic castle in tow, and plopped it right here on 5th Avenue."

I asked, "And the Sword means Arthur is back?"

"That was the prophecy, that Arthur Pendragon, the Once and Future King, would return, when the world needs him most desperately."

Lord Feathergrimm took his ink-drenched hanky and wrung drops back into the inkwell.

I said, "Merlin told us that Rat here is probably the new King Arthur."

Feathergrimm knocked the inkwell over. "Have you drawn Excalibur?" he asked Rat.

Rat blushed. He looked grimly down at his feet and mumbled, "Don't ask."

I caught Feathergrimm's eye and motioned 'Zip it.'

Feathergrimm fingered a stack of wrinkled old ink-stained books. He flipped their inky pages and said, "I shall keep searching for the 'skinny scoop.'"

Wishing Lord Feathergrimm luck, I held the library door open for Rat and Lily.

Out in the hallway, Merlin blocked our way.

"Time for class," he stated, grabbing Rat's collar.

"So, Mr. Merlin," Rat said, squirming, "what about this Morgan Le Fay dame? She still around? And what about that Mordred guy?"

Merlin froze.

Rat said, "Like, maybe he's the ghost that *isn't* haunting your castle."

The Magician shook Rat like a rat. "What's that?" Merlin screeched. "'Mordred,' you say? Mordred was a misunderstood hero."

Lily gasped. "But—" she said.

"You should learn more about him," Merlin continued, glaring at Rat. "Your next lesson shall be history."

I said, "But, I thought Mordred was a slimy snake-in-the-grass."

Merlin glared at me. "What does a janitor know about great men of history? Get to work!"

The old dust-bag had just the job in mind: scraping boogers and chewing gum from under desktops the rest of the afternoon.

Ah, detective work.

Chapter 10
Another Ghost?

Again, we waited until dark to look for the ghost.

Lily tagged along, and we stalked through the hallways and cavernous rooms of the ancient joint called Merlin's Institute.

Rat whispered, "Check out this door."

It was shiny bronze, ornately carved, mysterious in the red glow of the hall torches.

"Go in," Lily stated behind me. "Go on."

Rat opened the heavy door and we walked through.

"Dude," Rat gasped. "What the...?"

We stood outdoors, in full daylight, on a lakeshore at the foot of gargantuan granite mountains towering above.

A blue lake rippled in the golden sun.

On a stone floor facing the shore was...

A throne. A table. Banners hanging from stone walls. Shields, swords, and lances.

Lily walked through the display as if in a dream, whispering, "Ohmigod, ohmigod, ohmigod..."

She reached out, brushing the table reverently

with her fingers. "This is Arthur's Round Table."

Then there was a shimmering above the table. The glow grew and came into focus.

A wavy, misty guy floated just above us.

The guy wheezed, like a rusty Model T coughing to life.

Rat exclaimed, "Dude, how many ghosts do you *have* in this place?"

This was nothing like the terrifying Ghost Knight.

This was a shimmering weak old man.

The phantom's hair looked like it was hacked off by a push-mower.

His chin was covered with ragged, uneven stubble.

The ghost wore dirty, older than old-fashioned underwear.

Then the ghost spoke. "Wart?" A wheezy whisper. "Wart? Is it you?"

The three of us couldn't speak.

"Wart. Help me."

Rat snapped out of it.

"The name is Rat!" he barked and raised the wand.

The ghost faded away.

We stood there a moment, looking at each other with very puzzled 'hmmm???' expressions.

Rat said, "Who do you figure that was?"

"Dunno," I replied, "and I'm not sure we're gonna learn anything soon. We should search for the other ghost."

We returned to the grim torch-lit halls of the Institute. We gave it another two hours but turned up a total bunch of nothing.

Rat and Lily looked a little droopy, so we called it a night. We dropped Lily at the infirmary, to be near her dad. Rat and I headed for the basement.

"I can't take it in the dorm," Rat said. "Those princes are a bunch of whiners. Plus, Snotswarth keeps giving me the evil eyeball."

There was a loud CLUNK down the hall.

Then a fierce mechanical whisper, "Careful, knucklehead!"

I perked at that and whispered, "Is it the ghost?"

We crept forward and peeked around the corner.

Two brawny armored guards lugged a big crate, squeaking along the floor.

We crept quietly after them.

They entered a large storeroom.

Rat and I peeked in and saw some of Merlin's armored guards wrestling crates with crowbars.

One of them boomed out in a robotic voice, "Why's da boss so hot on gatherin' dese particular items?"

"I tole ya," another boom-boxed back. "We're gonna need all the serious armory we can get, for what's comin'."

"Yo," a guard squeaked, "check dis one out."

The goon in armor yanked an enormous two-handed axe out of a crate. The axe shined with some kind of weird energy.

Hot tamale! I pulled out my notebook to get some pics.

The guard swung the axe around. A jet of fire surged off the blade, blasting the plume of another guard's helmet in flames.

"Oops," the flame-thrower gulped and quickly tossed the axe on the stack.

The guard with the smoking plume-ash buzzed, "Why, I oughta," and clanged menacingly toward the flame-throwing goon.

A guard growled, "Break it up. Dis ain't no pillow fight. Da Boss said no messin' wid dis stuff."

"Yeah," the squeaky guy squawked, "we gotta be ready when the kid pulls the Sword."

"So," one of the guards grunted as he lifted a huge crate onto another, "why can't the kid pull the Sword?"

"Dunno," robot-voice buzzed, "but I tink sump'n's wrong wid 'im. Moronical or sump'n."

Rat sputtered and raised the wand.

I grabbed his arm.

Rat grumbled, "But that moron called me a moron."

"Drop it."

As we crept away, I muttered, "What's with all the scary weapons? I gotta bad feeling in the pit of my yolk. Can't say I like it."

Chapter 11
Pass de Dukes

Next morning, we stood in the hallway, just outside Lily's basement apartment. I jammed my head in the janitor's closet, trying to look busy. Somehow knowing what (or who) was coming next.

"Ah, Arthur, there you are." Merlin appeared suddenly around the corner.

"The name's Rat," said Rat.

"Whatever you say," Merlin said. "You're the king.

"I've decided," the old wizard said, "that what you need, Arthur, are better manners and a bit of culture.

"When you act more like a real prince, I'm sure you'll have no trouble drawing the Sword. Come along."

He glared at me and snapped, "Get to work!"

Firmly gripping Rat's shoulder, he marched off.

Lily and I followed quietly.

I hoped Rat didn't bite the old geezer. But, then again, I sorta hoped he would.

Merlin's "bit of culture" turned out to be dance class.

I went to work polishing the wall-sized mirrors in the back of the class. My excuse to hang around.

Rat looked at his dance outfit and whispered harshly, "You gotta be kiddin' me!"

Lily wore an old patched leotard and tutu.

The instructor wore a pink tutu around his broad and massive waist; dance tights of blinding purple; the cutest, most delicate pink slippers; and a gigantic armored knight's helmet!

"Po-sis-shun, uh…"

Another goon with a mechanical voice.

He pulled a book from his waistband. He opened it to a page: "Exercise 23: Pas De Deux."

He boomed, " ...'PASS De DUKES.'"

His voice again boomed, "'Da Dukes.' Is dat like, uh, 'Put up yer Dukes?'" He chortled.

Another voice I could almost recognize, but couldn't, electronic as it was.

'Who are these guys?' I thought, yanking out my notebook, and pressing 'RECORD' all in one move.

The gorilla in tights punched his elbow against a button on the wall.

Music blared out of large speakers, and the gorilla bounded around the dance floor, his helmet's visor clunking.

The instructor bounced over to Rat and yelled, "Dance, ya brat!"

Rat glared at the instructor, then glared at me.

Then Rat danced a couple of crazy, awkward moves—

and crashed right into the instructor!
The top-heavy teacher
toppled like a sack,
and his helmet
popped off!

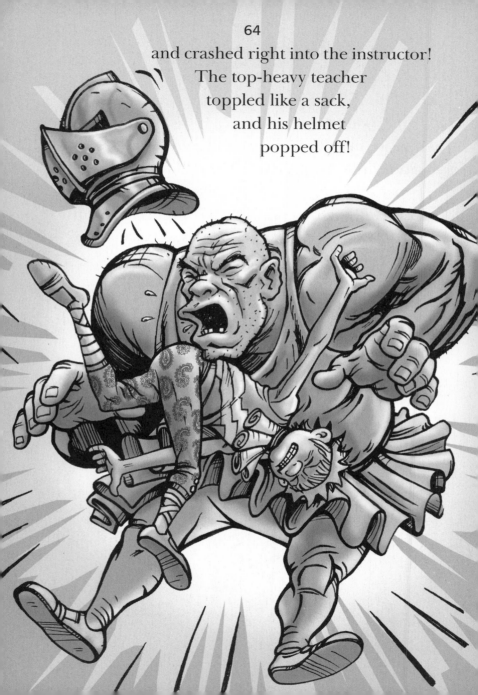

It was Knock-Out Louie!

The gangster.

Of the Potty Mouth Gang!

In a leotard?!

All of a sudden, like iron dominoes, every suit of armor I'd seen, or heard, in the joint fell into place.

Toothless Moe.

Lunky Larry.

One-Eyed Curly.

The Potty Mouth Gang.

"Royal" Flush's outfit.

"Oi!" Knock-Out Louie yelped, and I recognized Louie's regular, talking-gorilla Bonx voice.

The helmet lay at my feet.

I picked it up and put it on. "Hey, Bub," I squawked in an electronic buzz. "How ya doin'?"

I tossed the helmet to Louie. "Catch."

This was big.

Maybe too big.

Maybe it was time to visit a certain cop.

The one cop tough enough to take out the Potty Mouth gang (and maybe grab Boss Flush), once and for all.

Chapter 12
No Flushing Flush

"But, Lieutenant," I exploded, waving my notepad crammed with evidence in the air, "we can FLUSH 'Royal' Flush! You have to!"

Lieutenant Rosebriar snorted and huffed, his razor-sharp rhino horn dangerously zagging two inches from my face.

He snuffed, "'I have to,' 'I need to,' 'I got to!' This is all I get from the Police Commissioner. The Press!

"What I GOT to do," Rosebriar bellowed, "is NOT mess with Boss Flush until I have an AIR-TIGHT case. No 'Ifs, Ands, or BUTT-OWSKIs,' Dumpty. We still don't even know who Flush is."

"But," I persisted, "I think 'Royal' Flush is putting the squeeze on Merlin. Some kind of blackmail.

"Either Merlin coughs up, or The Armored Potty Mouth Tin-Can Goon Squad will personally squish him back to the Dark Ages!!

"Lieutenant, it fits. Merlin's students are loaded. Most of 'em royalty."

Rosebriar sat on the edge of his desk. I heard its familiar metallic groan and wondered how much longer it would hold up.

"So, you're telling me," said Rosebriar, "that one of the greatest wizards in history can't protect himself from a few muscle-bound dopes? It doesn't add up."

"I got a feeling," I started, but Rosebriar cut me off.

"Leave your feelings at the door, Dumpty."

"You're right, but it seems like the students are under lock and key. At the Institute."

Rosebriar grunted. "Got a ransom note? Anyone file charges?"

"No, but listen." I hit the notebook's 'PLAY' button.

A gargling buzz: "Dat's right! De udder way!" Rosebriar snorted.

"Wait, that's the wrong part!" I scrambled for another file. "What about this?"

I played back the Incident of the Flaming Plume.

"Is this a joke?!" Rosebriar rumbled.

"See? That big pile of magical weapons in the basement?"

Rosebriar hollered, "Are you kidding me? This is Merlin we're talking about! He's been guarding Excalibur for a decade. In the Files of All Known Weaponry, that Sword is Top Dog!

" Look at it this way, this city's probably a whole lot safer if Merlin did clear the cutlery off the streets!"

I stated, "But now they're in the hands of The Potty Mouth Gang! Listen to this!"

I turned my notepad on 'PLAY' and cranked up the volume:

"Dance, ya brat!"

Rosebriar roared, "So what? Even if it is Knock-Out Louie, I can't arrest 'im for wearing a tutu! Now get outta here!"

Chapter 13
"There Are No Ghosts"

I hauled shell back to the Institute.

I'd confront Merlin and yank the truth out of him, whisker by painful whisker.

I got to the Institute, picked up the kids, and headed for Merlin's office.

"Whaaaa…?" Merlin sputtered.

I smoothed my trench coat, stroked my mustache, and stated, "I know 'Royal' Flush is putting the squeeze on you. I can help!"

Merlin backed up from my nose and snorted, "So! It's you? You're better at cleaning toilets, Dumpty, than solving mysteries. I demanded you stay out of Institute business."

"I'm here on Princess Lily's Business," I said.

By now I'd backed the old geezer into a suit of armor.

"So, spill it, Maestro. What gives with the canned gorillas crawling everywhere?"

Merlin's eyes blazed like a nuclear furnace.

"And there's another ghost!" Rat said. "Here, in the school."

"Prattle," Merlin said.

"It's true," Lily said. "He's an old man calling for help. Calling 'Wart!'"

"'Wart'?" Merlin blustered. "'Wart'? Usually ghosts are searching for their heads! There ARE no ghosts at my Institute."

"Here's a clue," Rat snapped, "we just fought one. And if you got one ghost, you can have two. And, Mister Magician, you got two."

"Enough," Merlin said. Glaring at me, the ancient wizard stepped closer. "I shall relish watching my guards throw you out on your shell."

Rat cried, "'Relish'? With mustard?"

I said, "Don't worry. I'm leavin'."

I was out the door and down the hall before the wizard could say anything else.

Rat followed. "You're giving up?" he asked.

"I said I was leaving," I called loudly, as I turned a corner. Then I whispered, "But I didn't say when."

I hid in Lily's basement pad and caught forty winks until night, when I'd need all my wits, for sure.

Chapter 14
Ghost Busted

That night, we headed to the 5th floor.

"All set?" I said.

We hadn't taken three steps when, rounding a corner, we bumped into the ghastly glowing thing itself.

Rat hollered, "Duck!" He blasted a lightning bolt at the ghost.

Lily ducked for cover behind a stone pillar.

The knight staggered, lightning sparking and crackling on his armor.

Hold the phone!

The ghost was sucking up every ounce of Rat's spell like some crazy vacuum cleaner, and moaning, "More…magic…"

The flagstones vibrated with the ghost's heavy tread. What the—?

This time, the knight was solid, not the phantom who walked through walls, and magic-proof to boot. This time, Rat's blast made him stagger. That meant *I* could make him stagger.

I rolled at the towering monstrosity in my famous "Bowling-Ball Juggernaut POW."

The ghost pointed its "flashlight" at me, and jagged lightning zapped out.

YIKES!

I spun away as the electric bolt exploded the stone wall next to me into gravel.

Lily screeched.

Rat shouted, "Sha-Boom!"

Again the ghost absorbed the spell.

Then the ghost zapped me right in the face.

Next thing I knew, I was looking up at a very giant ghost and a giant Rat.

Hold on. *They* weren't giant-sized!
I was dinkier than a hummingbird's egg!

The ghost stomped. I rolled crazily out of the way.

His boot was a colossal slab of steel, crushing the flagstones beside me.

Rat zapped another spell.

The ghost soaked it up like it was starving.

Rat staggered.

Looming closer, the ghost moaned, "Where's my magic? My magic!"

And then, even more chilling, the ghost howled, "GIVE ME THE SWORD! OR DIE!"

The ghastly voice almost cracked my teeny shell.

Rat crumpled.

The ghost glared down at Rat's unmoving form.

His electric humming increased.

Then the ghost spun and strode away, like a passing lightning storm, down the ancient hallway.

Chapter 15
"Stupid, Stupid Boy"

Next morning, Rat lay in an infirmary cot, pale and weak.

I was still smaller than a chocolate egg, sitting on the blanket covering Rat's chest.

Lily sat beside her father on the cot next to us.

Nurse Punnymanny, placing her furry rabbit paw on Rat's forehead, said, "'E's right, alright. Temp's normal."

Rat mumbled, "What happened?"

"Well," I began, "we were fighting the ghost, and you conked out. Nurse Punnymanny and Lily brought us here."

Lily said, looking down, "You were really brave. Fighting the ghost."

Rat blushed.

She muttered, "I sure wasn't much help, though."

"Well," Rat said, "it's not your fault. Girls are just no good in a fight."

"Hey," I said. "Some of the toughest fighters I know are women."

I turned to Lily. "Don't listen to him. I know you don't want to hurt anyone. That's not something to be ashamed of. Plus, that was the first time you saw the ghost." Lily shrugged.

"Where's the wand?" Rat cried.

"Hidden under your pillow."

He pulled out our magic wand.

"It was weird," Rat said. "The ghost is a copycat."

"Whaddya mean?"

"Well, whatever spell I used—my lightning spell, my new shrink spell—he just shot it right back."

Rat grinned at me and said, "You look funny. Maybe we should call you 'Shrimpty' Dumpty from now on."

It was good to see he was feeling better. I said, "Quit kidding around and change me back."

But, just as Rat started with, "Sha—", who should come barging into the infirmary, but the walking laundry bag himself, Merlin.

I ducked deep into Rat's pocket.

"Why are you lollygagging in here, lad?" he stormed, striding over to Rat. "It's time to draw the Sword. Come along."

The headmaster spun, dragging poor Rat out by the ear. In Rat's pocket, I grew dizzy with the motion.

We jounced down and down the steps and swooped through the corridors to where the Sword stood.

Excalibur glowed dimly.

Merlin shoved us toward the stone. "Draw it, boy," Merlin said. "You're the king."

As Rat stepped up, the Sword's edge was almost right at the tip of my nose. Gulp.

I looked up at Rat yanking the hilt.

Nothing.

He yanked again. Same-o.

A big egg. Zilch. Zero.

Merlin screeched, "What is it? What are you doing wrong?" He stormed back and forth, shaking his head and stomping his feet.

"Stupid boy!" he screamed. "You're a...stupid, stupid boy."

"Dude," Rat whispered. He turned and slunk out.

We found Lily watching from the shadows just outside Merlin's office.

She whispered, "Sorry you couldn't draw Excalibur, Rat." She put her hand on his arm. He didn't seem to mind.

Rat said, "I'm getting tired of Old Moss-breath messin' with me. And," (he yanked me out of his pocket, glaring), "bad idea, Humpty, forcing me to be here. To be in school at all!"

"Okay, okay," I shouted in my 2-inch-loud voice. "Remember, we're doing all this for Balto and Lily. Now, get me back to normal."

One 'Sha-Boom' later, I was my full-size, hard-boiled detective self again.

Rat muttered, "We'll see who's 'stupid', old man," and stormed away. He called over his shoulder, "I just figured out who 'Wart' is."

Chapter 16
A Wart by Any Other Name

Rat took us to the library.

As we entered Lord Feathergrimm's domain, I looked at Rat, questioning.

Rat conspicuously jabbed his own cheek, mouthing, 'Wart'. Then he pointed at the librarian.

Rat snarled, "Okay, Professor Featherbrain! Spill it. You're the glowing ghost. I got you all figured out."

Lord Feathergrimm didn't even look up from the parchment he studied.

"Rat," I started, but he put his hand up and again pointed at his cheek. 'Wart! Wart!' he mouthed.

"Wart!" came a voice behind us.

Feathergrimm jerked his head up.

Lily and Rat and I spun.

The other ghost. The flickering old man glowed thinly, saying, "Wart?"

We all watched Feathergrimm walk around and through the shimmering specter.

"I can't make out..." Lord Feathergrimm mumbled. "If I could just see..." he said, stroking the thin air of the ghost's face.

The ghost, searching the spaces in front of him, moaned, "Wart. Help!"

Then, he softly faded.

Feathergrimm scratched his head, muttering, "It looks like...if only...it could just be...but that underwear!"

Rat said, "Why does the ghost keep calling me 'Wart'?"

The librarian answered, "If you are indeed the Once and Future King, then you're Arthur reborn. And 'Wart' was Arthur's nickname when he was a boy. It sort of rhymes with 'Art' for Arthur, you see and—"

I said, "'Wart'? Nickname?" The biggest lightning bolt that ever struck a noggin zapped me fried.

"Merlin should've known King Arthur's nickname," I said. "He was his teacher.

"So, either he really knows, and he's hiding it, or..."

"Or what?" Rat asked.

"He really doesn't know."

I handed the wand to Rat. "Lily. Stay here."

Rat and I tore out of the library. I said, "This could get rough. Be ready. For anything."

Chapter 17
Wand and Sword

Rat SHA-BOOMed a snoozer spell on the armored goons guarding Merlin's office.

For dramatic emphasis, I kicked the double doors open and rushed in.

Rat scurried beside me, wand held at the ready.

Merlin stood stiffly behind his desk.

"So this is your idea of 'leaving', is it?" Merlin asked. He glared with the angry, nuclear glow again.

I said, "Fess up—why don't you know who Wart is?

d," I continued, my steam definitely up, "I've never seen you do any magic. So, how did you do it?"

"Do what?" Merlin and Rat asked together.

"Get rid of the real Merlin," I said.

The wizard smiled. An evil, snake-like grin.

"Huh?" said Rat. "You mean...?"

Rat leapt on Merlin's desk, and full-force yanked the magician's beard.

Rat fell off the desk, Merlin's whiskers and face-mask ripping off with a sound like Velcro.

Standing before us was some guy I didn't know.

A skinny guy by the looks of his sunken cheeks.

A nervous guy, I could tell, from his twitching eyebrows, lips, and ears.

A sickly pale guy, with a sick grin on his sick face. Sick menace in his eyes.

"A phony Merlin," I said. "In a phony beard. Funny—when you yanked my mustache, it stayed on."

Rat (Mr. Shoot-First-and-Ask-Questions-Later) fired the wand. "SHA-BOOM!"

A lightning bolt crackled into the phony Merlin.

His robes blew off in tatters, revealing something metallic beneath. Something glowing.

The lightning skittered around the gleaming armor. Then the metal soaked up Rat's spell, a sponge absorbing spilled lemonade.

"Surprise!" said the glowing ghost.

He drew his flashlight-wand.

"Watch out, kid!" I dove for the maniac, but a lightning bolt jolted me.

I caught just the edge of it. Most of the magic blasted straight for Rat.

Rat brought the wand around like a ballplayer swinging for a fastball.

The lightning ricocheted off the wand, tore through the heavy curtains behind the phony Merlin, then slammed into the doors at the back of the office.

They blew apart in a fiery detonation.

"Your magic is useless against me," said Ghost Guy. "Your magic…is mine!"

The familiar burring, buzzing, tingling swept over my shell.

I wanted to lie down and sleep.

Rat was pale and shaking. He crumpled to his knees, trying to raise the wand.

"You don't have a chance," the glowing imposter said. "I beat Merlin, the greatest wizard of all time."

I could see the Sword in the stone behind him, a dark silhouette.

"Who are you?" I said, weakly. Maybe I could buy time, give Rat a chance to recover, somehow get the upper hand.

The Ghosty Guy smiled his sick, crazy smile. He swept a lock of his greasy black hair out of his eyes.

"I am Mordred," he said.

Chapter 18
The Full-of-Hot Heir

"You look pretty good for a dead guy, " I said.

"Fool," the crazy-man snarled. "I AM THE DESCENDENT OF THE BLOODLINE OF MORDRED!"

I said, "Hold the phone. Mordred, son of King Arthur?"

"None other," Mordred said. "I am MORDRED PENDRAGON, the 34th!"

Something about this crazy-eyed maniac looked familiar. How? Why? When?

I heard a gasp at the doorway.

"Lily," I cried. "I told you to wait in the library!"

"I want to help," Lily said. She stepped into the room, staring at Mordred.

Her face was stern, her eyes flashing. "Why did you hurt my poppa?"

Boy, she looked like her mom in the picture, standing there so regally poised.

Her mom! That's who Mordred reminds me of! What the…?

Mordred said, "Balto, the poor fool, got in my way. Nothing can stop me from getting Excalibur." He gestured toward the Sword. It glowed with soft light, sparking brighter and brighter.

I said, "Poor schmuck. You couldn't even draw the Sword."

"Excalibur is mine," Mordred screamed. "Mine by birthright."

His face twisted in frustration.

He pounded the desk.

"I swore the Sword would be mine. I needed a new plan. I am a scientific GENIUS. All I needed was time and money to fulfill my destiny!"

His ghostly armor glimmered and crackled.

"It took me years, but I finally created my armor. Armor that absorbs magical energy."

"So you're some kind of magic-sucking vampire?" I said.

"Crude," Mordred said. "I can take a wizard's magical energy and use it against him. I defeat him with his own spells. And suck most of the spell's energy."

"You're a walking flashlight battery," I said.

Mordred ignored me. He was totally absorbed in himself.

"Not since Morgan Le Fay has anyone bested the mighty Merlin. She imprisoned him in a crystal cave. I've done her one better."

Mordred pointed.

Beyond the blackened ruin of the doors Rat had blasted stood a large slab of crystal. It glowed with the same sickening light as Mordred's armor.

There were pipes and pulsing cables hooked up to the crystal.

Inside was a shape…a man's shape, tall and thin.

"Behold the once-mighty Merlin," Mordred said.

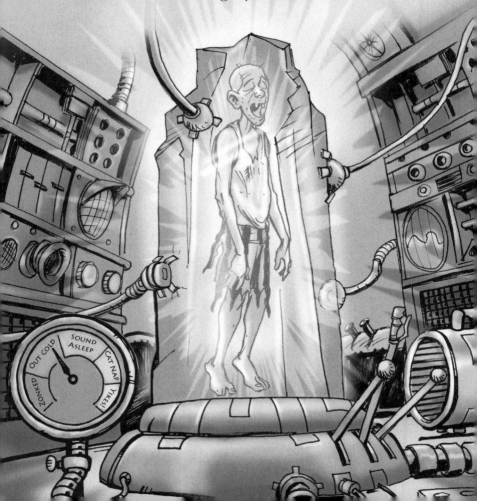

"So, why the ghost act?" I said. "How did you walk through walls?"

"There is nothing magic can do that science can't do better," said Mordred. "Sometimes I 'haunt' the castle myself. That's when I steal magical energy from the fools. But other times I use holograms. To frighten and confuse."

"But why?" Lily asked.

"It takes a lot of power to run my armor," Mordred said. "And lately," he gestured at Merlin imprisoned in the crystal, "the old fool seems to be fighting me somehow. Draining me.

"I needed more energy. So I took it from the princes here. Those spoiled brats! It was a pleasure to see them squirm in fear. To watch them faint as I absorbed their magic. Kept them prisoners in their own school."

I said, "So, you took over the Institute, and waited like a spider for a fly. Waited for the prince destined to free the Sword."

"Exactly," said Mordred. "And now, boy," he pointed his wand at Rat, "I've found you!"

I had to do something!

I yelled, "Mordred!" I gulped. "I challenge you... to a wizard's duel!"

Chapter 19
Another Secret

Did I even have the slightest clue what I was doing?

I stated, "Just let me grab my wand and I'll show you some real magic."

"We'll duel," Mordred said. "And Merlin will have some company in crystal."

I edged over to Rat.

He moaned, "What…I…" He was gasping for air.

"It's okay, kid," I said. "Just breathe." I felt tired too, but Rat had a lot more magic in him than I did, so I figured he was more sapped by Mordred.

I pulled the wand from his limp hand.

I spun and faced Mordred. "Okay, Buster," I said, furiously. "I'm gonna do what I swore to the Cloud Gnomes of Xanadu (who gave me this wand) I'd never do! Too dangerous!" I pulled up my trench coat sleeves and waved my wand in circles.

Mordred yawned.

I stated confidently, "I'm gonna use my 'Ultra-Strength Boo-Doo Doo-Doo' magic. A spell so powerful that no one's had the guts to use it… until now!"

"Fascinating," Mordred said with a smirk.

I twirled my wand all fancy, circling it in the air, tapping out impressive showers of magic sparks.

"A hooba-hoo," I shouted. I jumped around on one leg. "Hippity-hokey-pokey!" I spun around with a hop.

"Will this take long?" Mordred asked, bored.

"Hey," I said, "a big spell like this takes a serious build-up."

I went for the big finish, jumping, twisting, spinning, moving closer and closer to Mordred.

This had to work.

"Hey shimmy shammy with a fat whimmy whammy!" I shouted.

Mordred's wand crackled with all the magic power he'd stolen from Rat. "I'm ready," he exclaimed, taking his stance.

"Good," I shouted and SLAMMED my wand, hard, onto his.

His weapon spun from his grasp and I snatched it out of the air.

"NOOOOO!" Mordred screeched, lunging for me.

I head-butted him, and Mordred staggered.

"Without your wand," I said, "you're nothing but a skinny doofus in a tin can."

"Wrong, Egg!" Mordred snarled.

Then I heard the sound of knuckles cracking! Huge, hairy, barely-human knuckles. In armor.

Lily shrieked and ducked behind me.

"You need help, Boss Flush?" Toothless Moe's booming voice boom-boxed.

I spun, and found myself glaring at a door full of Potty Mouths—gargantuan armored knight hoods!

Knock-Out Louie carried an iron mace no smaller than a cast-iron stove.

More than twenty canned hoods clamored into the room like a clanking freight train.

"Perfect timing, Toothless," Mordred said. "And now, Egg-head, you learn my final secret. I am Mordred...and I am also 'Royal' Flush. The leader of the Potty Mouth Gang."

"Ulp."

Chapter 20
Once, and Future

I couldn't take all these guys! They were tough street fighters. I had the wand, but…

Mordred howled, "It is my destiny to wield Excalibur. No one can stop me!"

My best bet was to keep him talking.

"So," I casually stated, "you're the secret boss behind the biggest robberies in this town?"

"Certainly, I needed money to develop my armor," Mordred said. "Science is expensive. I've been poor all my life! And New Yolk owes me!

"It was delightful putting the squeeze on the mayor and his council. And all their businesses. And every joe on the corner. Squeeze them for all they've got!"

"So," I said, "you couldn't pull the Sword, but you wanted to rule anyway, huh? Is that why you're 'Royal'?"

Mordred snorted. "Life is a high-stakes poker game," he said. "And a Royal Flush beats everything! I own this city!

"When I gain Excalibur, then the fireworks will begin. I have an armed strike force ready to bring

New Yolk City to its knees. Then on and on, one city after another, until my army takes over the continent. Then I, the glorious king wielding Excalibur, will rule the WORLD!"

I flashed a glance at the Sword in the stone. My brain was itching, like Excalibur was trying to tell me something.

"You want we should scramble him?" Knock-Out Louie asked.

"I want him pounded into powdered egg," said Mordred.

Louie swung his giant mace.

Moe swung his magical flaming axe.

Yikes! I barely spun out of the way.

Time to try the wand.

"Sha-Boom!" I shot out my best attempt at a shrink spell over the lot of 'em. Instead of shrinking the attacking mob, my spell only managed to spew a lovely shower of skunk spray.

"Ulp." A 'stink' spell.

Louie covered his face with his arm. "P.U.!! Who cut the cheese?" The goons frantically waved the air, weapons slashing everywhere.

The stink slowly faded away, and Knock-Out Louie stormed over. "You still want we should pummel 'im to powder now, Boss?"

"No," Mordred crooned, "changed my mind. Chop him into egg salad!"

Toothless Moe bellowed, "Who's got mayo?"

"Wait, wait," I shouted.

Rat was trying to get to his feet. He still looked white and shaky.

Sorry, kid, for what I was about to do.

"Rat," I called, pointing at him. "It's time to draw the Sword, and destroy these flunkies!"

Mordred screamed fiercely, "Don't let him near the Sword. Not yet!"

Rat didn't even have time to blink before a football-team's worth of armored hoodlums dove on him.

I grabbed Lily and pulled her to the Sword.

"Lily," I whispered fiercely. "Draw the Sword."

"What?" Lily gasped. "The Sword? But Rat?"

"You gotta do it!" I encouraged her.

Lily. The Sword. Glowing every time Rat got close
to it. But, every time, Lily was with Rat.

And just a few moments ago, the Sword had been
dark…until Lily got here!

Lily, whose mother looked like Mordred.

Lily, who has a family ring with a dragon emblem.

I'd almost missed it: who says the Once and Future
King has to be a boy?

Princess Lily stood there, hesitant, reaching for Excalibur.

She grasped the hilt.

Taking a deep breath, she pulled at the Sword. Smoothly, cleanly, with a ringing CLING, Excalibur came free of the stone!

Mordred whirled. "No! Impossible."

Toothless Moe bellowed, "Hardy-har, Boss. Don't sweat it. Dis puny peanut can't do diddley, even wid thirty swords."

Mordred laughed. "Give me Excalibur, janitor's daughter. You're unworthy."

With a wily sneer, he strode toward Lily.

I dove at Mordred. Knock-Out Louie smashed his mace in front, blocking me.

Snarling like ravenous hyenas, Mordred and several thugs closed in on Lily.

Her back was now to the wall. Trapped.

Princess Lily lifted Excalibur.

"I don't want to hurt anyone," Lily cried out. She looked at me and Rat in our desperate trouble. "I'm...I'm just going to help my friends."

Lily raised the Sword higher. Excalibur glowed brighter and brighter. The light shattered into a thousand sunbeams. It drowned Lily in its brilliance.

Before our startled peepers, Lily changed. The Sword changed.

Liquid steel crept up her arm like vines, growing from the Sword. The steel encased her hands, her arms, all the way up her body and down her legs.

In armor. Bright, glittering armor.

Lily's face was hidden by a fierce dragon helmet.

She grasped Excalibur and stepped forward. She radiated dangerous power.

In a voice that was Lily's, but also wasn't, the figure spoke: "We are...Excalibur!"

We all froze, staring at the glowing silver figure.

What had Mordred said about Excalibur? 'There's never been a weapon like it'?

"G-get her, boys!" Mordred croaked.

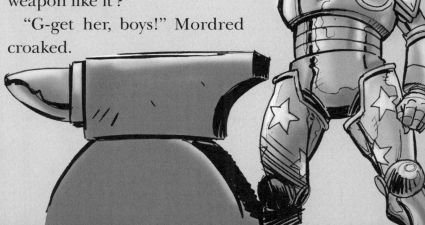

But Lily didn't hurt a soul. She dented a few noggins with the flat of her Sword, but never stabbed or cut.

She twirled Mordred, the Once and Future Wimp, till he turned green.

Slowly, the steel creature morphed into our soft-faced, gentle Princess Lily again.

She wobbled and leaned against the stone. "Whoa," she panted.

Rat said, wobbly himself, "Wicked."

The sound of wheezing reached us from the crystal of Merlin's prison.

Then, a voice: "Wart. Help me, Wart!"

Lily looked at the figure trapped in the crystal.

"I…I guess I'm Wart," she said. She smashed the prison full-force.

The shattering gemstone sprayed the room with chunks of glowing crystal.

The skinny guy in old underwear stumbled out of the smoke and crystal debris.

This was Merlin.

He had this aura of terrific power.

His eyes held the wisdom of centuries.

Even with no beard and wearing raggedy long-johns, you could tell he was the real deal.

The befuddled wizard gazed blankly around his office. "God's whiskers," he muttered. "This place is a mess."

Rat looked at the ancient magician, and admiringly said, "Man, this is one crazy school. And that's the place for me."

Chapter 21
The Queen

Lieutenant Rosebriar huffed and snuffled as he snapped the cuffs on "Royal" Flush and rounded up the Potty Mouth Gang.

"Gotta say, Dumpty," the lieutenant bellowed, "this time you didn't gum it all up."

That's the closest I'll get to a compliment from Lieutenant Rosebriar.

And Rosebriar, with great satisfaction, dragged Mordred's skinny carcass (a patrolman toting his ghost armor) to the paddy wagon and zoomed off.

On returning to Merlin's office, we found the wizard robed again, his beard full and hair long.

Merlin, Lily, and Prince Balto visited quietly by the stone. Nurse Punnymany towered over the group.

Balto, thin and pale, held his daughter close.

He smiled at us.

Dugal Farthing and some of the other princes scrambled to see the new celebrity.

I said, "So Lily's the new King Arthur, huh?"

Merlin looked bewildered. "Ahem…that is…so it seems," Merlin said. "Excalibur."

"Weren't expecting a girl?" I asked.

"I'm over a thousand years old," Merlin said. "I'm a little old-fashioned. Mordred did me a great favor. He was the one who admitted Lily into the Institute. I was focusing so hard on finding a king that I almost overlooked our Queen…" His voice faded.

Lily shyly smiled.

"Well, this should be interesting for everyone then," I said.

Excalibur glowed brightly. Lily lifted the Sword, puzzled. Somewhere, in between the shimmering lights of the Sword, we began to make out…

Rat, in awe, whispered, "Not another ghost!"

But it was.

A glittering shade of a young, pretty woman, dressed as a queen.

Balto gasped, "It…can't be…" He stumbled back and slumped against the wall.

"Poppa?" Lily ran to him.

The ghost followed.

"Interesting," said Merlin.

Lily stared at the vision, wide-eyed.

The vision spoke. "Look how you've grown." Ghostly hands reached toward Lily.

The ghost said, "It's me. Your mom!"

Lily's eyes grew wider. She slumped down next to her father.

"Gwyneth?" Balto whispered. "How…"

"I've come for Lily's Coronation," the ghost said softly. "All the Pendragons get to come."

"Ah," said Merlin.

"Pen…dragon?" Lily said.

"Honey, this Mordred, who you defeated today, is my older brother." The ghost wrinkled her nose in disgust. "He was always a cruel bully.

"My whole family was cruel. Always blabbing on about their bloodline and family history. But they totally ignored our ancestor Arthur, who they believed was a weak fool. They started counting the generations from Mordred. As if being descended from him was anything to be proud of! My brother was the worst!"

Gwyneth placed her transparent hand on Lily's.

"Even as a young kid, Mordred was a devious criminal, and a gifted scientist. He pulled all kinds of robberies and jewel heists, blackmail. And he always got away with it!

"I finally ran away when I was seventeen. I only took one thing with me when I left. Arthur's ring."

Lily gasped and drew out her ring on its chain.

"That's the Pendragon," Gwyneth whispered, tracing a ghostly finger along the dragon on Lily's ring.

Gwyneth reached out toward the prince. "Then I met dear Balto. I never told him anything. I couldn't." She turned back to Lily, "I'm so proud of you."

I shook my head and blinked. The walls of the office seemed to fade away; we stood suddenly outside, but not on the Institute Grounds.

We stood in an old, old forest.

The green surrounding us was too green for modern eyes. A green that doesn't exist anymore.

I poked Rat and said, "Do you see that?"

Moving slowly through the dense trees and dappled by the leafy light, arrived dozens of...

"What? Who?" asked Rat, his jaw dropping.

"Ghosts."

They were more than outlines, but made of lines thin as cobweb.

"Ghosts," Rat said, breathless.

These ghosts were all dressed in:

Long robes;

Suits of armor;

Crowns, jewelry, and lances.

Queen Gwyneth and Prince Balto stood on either side of their daughter.

Merlin spoke in a full, rich voice as each ghost approached Princess Lily and knelt:

"Queen Guenevere of Camelot."

I whispered, "Good-lookin' dame."

Rat whispered, "Yeah. All shiny."

"Sir Lancelot du Lac."

His face looked like an ugly rock with chiseled eyes.

"Sir Gawain…"

Each and every Knight of the Round Table was there.

And then, every ghost turned and raised sword, lance, and kerchief:

"The Once and Future King, Arthur Pendragon!"

A bent, weathered ghost stepped before Lily.

The king was actually pretty young when Mordred killed him. I guess he just looked old, bowed with cares.

Arthur weakly bent his knee.

He said in a gravelly voice, "Your Majesty."

A figure lurked on the shadowy outskirts of the crowd. A young man with black hair and burning eyes. He wore black armor, and it looked like there was a gash in the breastplate.

The figure turned away into the forest, and vanished.

'Hmm,' I wondered. 'The first Mordred?'

King Arthur slowly, shakily, raised his hands to his head. I saw, on his ghostly right hand, the ghost-ring of the Pendragon.

He removed his ghost-crown, and placed it on Lily.

The shade of Arthur slowly wafted away.

"All hail Princess Lily," Merlin cried. "Our Once and Future Queen."

All the ghosts shouted, "Huzzah! Huzzah!" and then slowly faded away along with the forest.

Gwyneth smiled happily at Queen Lily then paled to nothingness.

We were back in Merlin's office.

I noticed Lily's new crown was now solid, gleaming.

Rat said, "So, Your Highness, where's your kingdom? Hey, I just heard there's a job in the Mayor's Office!" He snickered.

"Hmmmm," said Merlin. "That may be a good place for the new queen to begin her reign. The Sword Excalibur appears when humanity needs it most. The world is certainly in dire straits these days, and that's a fact.

"New Yolk City itself must play an important role in the future of all mankind."

Lily said, "The new Camelot?"

Merlin replied, "Indeed."

Rat said, "Not too much pressure, huh?"

"But what if I can't do it?" Lily asked.

I said, "Figure it this way—King Arthur's reign busted up after the battle against Mordred. And, now, your reign jump-starts, and you've already slam dunked that ugly business. You won. Sounds like you're the Big Cheese to me."

Rat slapped her on the back. "Chill, Queenie-girl. You'll be super!"

Then he snapped to attention, saluted, and said, "I'm calling you, 'The Once and Future Wart.'"

Lily giggled, for the first time since we met her.

Epilogue

And that's how it played out. Merlin took Lily down to City Hall, and Lily flashed the Sword. There'd been so much mess around there lately, with the arrests and all, everyone was glad to dump all the problems into someone's lap.

So Lily (with Merlin looking over her shoulder) is our new Mayor.

New Yolk went all out and embraced Queen Lily Pendragon, the Sword, the whole shebang.

The city threw a parade.

Before Rat and I knew it, we were swept up by the crowd. "Major Excellent," Rat screeched, as we plopped onto a horse-drawn Royal Carriage.

The weather in New Yolk City was gorgeous!

Lily, holding Excalibur, was first-class beautiful, in her shiny crown and big, happy smile.

She waved at the crowd, and gazed at her dad. Balto stood next to her, dressed to the hilt in his classy duds.

Merlin, Rat, and I shared the bumper seat at the back of the Coach of Honor.

Rat said, "That wraps up another case. Write it down, Humpty: 'The Mystery of Merlin and the Once and Future Wart'."

I chuckled. "Better just make it, 'The Mystery of Merlin and the Gruesome Ghost.' Don'tcha think?"

"Whatever."

I shouted over to Merlin, "Thanks for letting Rat into your school!"

"I'm sure it will be…most fascinating," said Merlin, glancing at Rat. The old wizard's eyes sparkled.

"So that's one problem down," I said. "But let me ask you this: How did you transport your entire castle here? How did we get into that old forest? And, most importantly, how am I gonna get Rat to take a bath?"

Merlin chuckled and said, "There are some mysteries, my dear egg-head, not even you will ever solve."

Case Closed!

Nate Evans has illustrated over 35 books, and written a few, too, including several picture books co-authored with Laura Numeroff. The latest of these is the *New York Times* Bestseller *The Jellybeans and the Big Dance*, illustrated by Lynn Munsinger. Nate currently lives in Georgia with his wonderful wife and three goofy dogs.

Paul Hindman lives in Boulder, Colorado. He has been scribbling stories ever since he learned how to write in 2nd Grade.

His works have been published by Random House (*Dragon Bones*), aired on PBS (*Zoobilee Zoo*), and distributed by Warner Brothers (*Rainbow Brite and the Star-Stealer*).

Paul spent much of his childhood in Seoul, Korea, and Bangkok, Thailand, as well as many other exotic lands like Denton, Texas.

Vince Evans started his artistic training by copying his big brother Nate's drawings. Vince has worked for numerous comic and book companies, and has won the Spectrum Silver Award for excellence in comic art. This book marks the first professional collaboration with his brother.

Existing solely on a diet of instant coffee and kidney beans, Vince lives with his beautiful wife Laurie and has two dogs that have been trained to beg editors to extend deadlines and bark when he falls asleep while working.